P9-BII-126

This book is given with love:

_____

_____

Copyright © 2018 by Puppy Dogs & Ice Cream, Inc.
All rights reserved. Published in the United States by Puppy Dogs & Ice Cream, Inc.
ISBN: 978-1-949474-30-5
Edition: June 2019

For all inquiries, please contact us at:
info@puppysmiles.org

To see more of our books, visit us at:
www.PuppyDogsAndIceCream.com

WRITTEN BY
Jason Kutasi

ILLUSTRATED BY
Javier Gimenez Ratti

— THE GREAT —
Bear Brigade

BIG BUBBLE TROUBLE!

The Great Bear Brigade has lots of stories to share.
Once you read their adventures then you'll be aware,
Of life lessons to learn and how to take care.
They will help you live smart and always beware!

If you've been playing outside,
and get mud on your shirt...

You can jump in the bathtub,
to wash off the dirt.

Fill it with bubbles,
and build a great moat...

It will be really cool,
to see everything float.

Bathtime will be fun, as you clean off the rubble...

But now you find yourself trapped
in a giant soapy bubble...

You start floating too high,
and now you're in trouble...

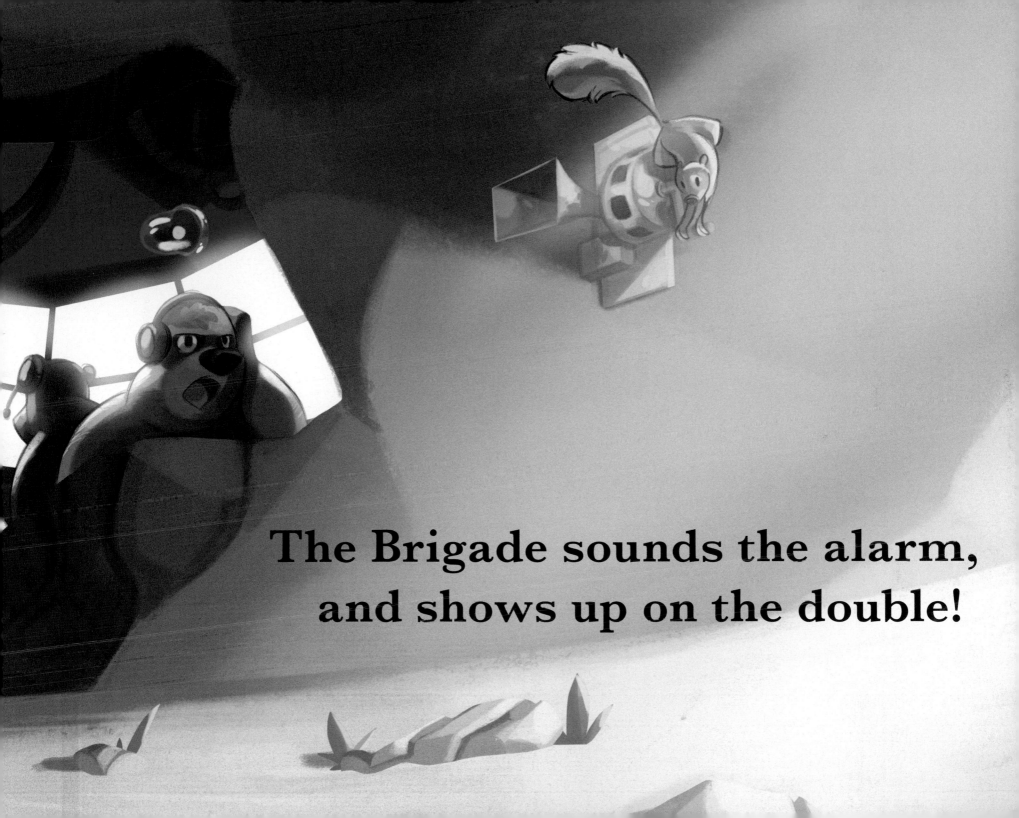

The Brigade sounds the alarm,
and shows up on the double!

The bears will solve the whole problem, and not just a fraction...

They'll figure out a solution,
and then go into action...

Should your big bubble burst,
you'll get a quick reaction.

The Bears' words of advice
are a really good bet...

Always tell an adult
before you get wet...

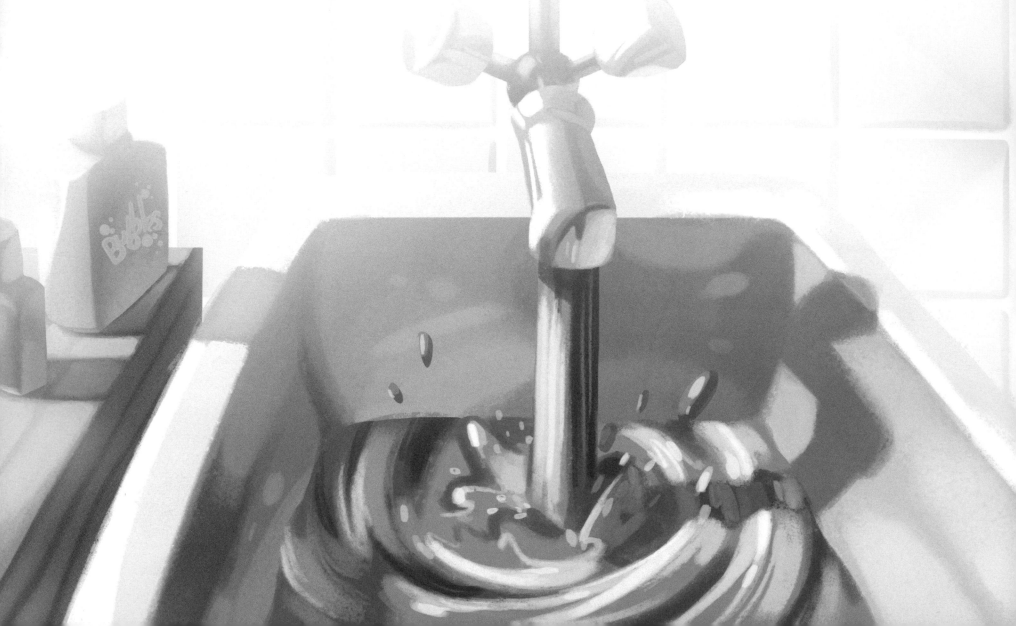

Watch out for big bubbles,
and then you are set!

The Great Bear Brigade is simply the best.
  When they sense you're in trouble, they'll never rest,
And all of their skills will be put to the test.
  They're happy to help, and they do it with zest!

♥ Claim Your FREE Gift!

Visit ➡ PDICBooks.com/bearbubble

Thank you for purchasing The Great Bear Brigade: Big Bubble Trouble, and welcome to the Puppy Dogs & Ice Cream family.

We're certain you're going to love the little gift we've prepared for you at the website above.